I0530593

I took one last shot at dissuading Sally from visiting Ghost Lady. "Tom's going to the church picnic this afternoon," I said, doing my best to put on an impish grin. "You wouldn't want to miss him."

"You don't know anything about boys," Sally said.

"What if he doesn't wait? He might leave early."

She shrugged. "It'd be his loss."

Charlotte's Cove
Copyright © 2015 Scott T. Barnes
All rights reserved
Published by New Myths Publishing
www.NewMythsPublishing.com

ISBN: 978-1-939354-02-0

Cover art:
Copyright © David McGrath, used by permission

Cover and interior design © 2015 Knotted Road Press

Never miss a release!
If you'd like to be notified of new releases, sign up for my newsletter.

I only send out newsletters once a quarter, will never spam you, or sell your information to a third party. You can also unsubscribe at any time.

http:// www.NewMythsPublishing.com/Newsletter

This book is licensed for your personal enjoyment only. All rights reserved. This is a work of fiction. All characters and events portrayed in this book are fictional, and any resemblance to real people or incidents is purely coincidental. This book, or parts thereof, may not be reproduced in any form without permission.

Charllote's Cove

SCOTT T. BARNES

New Myths Publishing
www.NewMythsPublishing.com

Also By Scott T. Barnes

Charlotte's Cove
Insect Sculptor
The Fey Prison Warden

Introduction

Several years ago a friend and I spent a week visiting Nova Scotia, traveling through the wild countryside, admiring the storm-wracked landscape, watching in awe as the ocean blasted through narrow bays. In the Bay of Fundy the tide drops over 50 feet, and the power of the water washing out to sea is awesome to behold. We met many wonderful people in the local pubs and bed-and-breakfasts. We heard many local legends. I have since read more.

Few other places on earth are as beautiful as Nova Scotia. No other place could be more sea-haunted.

Camping on Brier Island on a stormy night inspired me to write, "Charlotte's Cove." The wind whipped sparks from our driftwood fire away into the night. The rain pelted our tent. The sea howled.

I will never forget it.

Captain Alison Osinski helped me with the nautical sections of this story.

"Charlotte's Cove" is named after my grandmother, Charlotte Mathis. I dedicate this to her.

Charllote's Cove

We skirted the Mi'Kmaq graveyard and cut through a briar hedge rather than take Fool's Chance Lane and risk being seen. Charlotte's Cove is a white, clapboard town built around a wharf where the fishing vessels moor and the swells of the North Atlantic roll in restless blue. The waterfront holds eateries, public washrooms, a general store with two gas pumps, and a post office.

Three roads spoke outwards to a semi-circle with blue shuttered fishermen's cottages where stacks of lobster traps, worn lines and gathered driftwood smother feeble lawns and the Nova Scotia Lutheran Church stands watch with granite sentinels. On the third ring rest the smaller, neater houses of government employees and widows.

Beyond that lies Moody Manor.

I took one last shot at dissuading Sally from visiting Ghost Lady. "Tom's going to the church picnic this afternoon," I said, doing my best to put on an impish grin. "You wouldn't want to miss him."

"You don't know anything about boys," Sally said.

"What if he doesn't wait? He might leave early."

She shrugged. "It'd be his loss."

I bit my lip and scurried to catch Sally's stride. Folks here feared Ghost Lady and her witching, and they certainly didn't approve of kids going up to Moody Manner where she lived and filling their heads with strange ideas. But I wanted very badly to be friends with Sally. She was a tomboy with beautiful, golden locks and a quick wit. She seemed to know all the secrets in the universe. Besides, she was fourteen, five years older than me.

What her obsession with Ghost Lady was, I'll never know. They seemed to be kindred spirits, wild and alone, wispy boned like cattail naiads, with one foot in this world and one beyond.

I caught my breath when I saw Ghost Lady on the front porch, dressed all in black and seesawing in a rocking chair. Moody Manor's blue paint flaked off in great vertical stripes. Lord Chester H. Moody, famous Indian killer in the French and Indian Wars, built it in 1772. The Manor overlooked Charlotte's Cove on one side and Kloqntiej Head on the other, where the waves roared through Kloqntiej Blowhole, sending up great plumes of white like the Devil's smoke.

Ghost Lady waved us over. A dead chicken hung over the porch, its blood dried on the stoop. Little bones lay scattered in a pie tin. I knew she had looked into the future.

I held Sally's hand and she squeezed mine back; it was warm and I was okay.

"You brought someone to meet me," Ghost Lady said.

"I came to hear the story," Sally replied.

"My name's Mary-Anne," I said, earning an elbow from Sally. We'd met several times, but Ghost Lady seemed awfully old – maybe she forgot.

"You shouldn't have brought her, Sally. She isn't like us. No Narnia fauns in Mary-Anne's wardrobe, no three-wish lamps in musty attics or enchanted horses on merry-go-rounds, only biology books and sextets and such."

"You promised you'd tell me the end," Sally said. She pulled up a second rocker and I sat between them on an old, yellow ice chest that smelled like rotten scallops – I wouldn't have peeked inside for anything. "I want to hear how Pajdoobaachk got his bride."

"Pajdoobaachk, son of Mi'kmaq chief Camsogoochech. That tale spans many years."

Sally leaned forward eagerly. "They had just had a wedding feast and Pajdoobaachk married Quispamsis, daughter of a neighboring tribe."

"Was he a rogue like Tom?" I asked, earning another elbow.

"He was sailing to Gull Island with Quispamsis to consummate," Sally said, "but he didn't make a sacrifice."

I frowned and filed that word away to ask about later; right then I didn't want to interrupt. We could barely see the sand bar called Gull Island through the haze, but I knew from history that the Mi'kmaq Indians sailed out there and farther, even several hundred miles to Newfoundland in nothing more than masted canoes.

"That's right," Ghost Lady said. "The year was 1734. Pajdoobaachk scorned Leviathan, who the Mi'kmaq called the Giant Whale, and nothing angers the gods more than when people think they are above them."

"What happened?" I asked. "Did he kill Pajdoobaachk?"

"Leviathan is too cruel for that."

"Pajdoobaachk sailed with his bride," Sally said, "and a whirlpool formed in front of them. Wherever he turned the whirlpool followed. The Sky spirit blew hard, trying to blow them to safety, but Leviathan threw the sea against them."

Ghost Lady, whose real name was Bea Clements, pulled her shawl closer around her shoulders. "A pod of porpoises paced alongside," she said.

"They tried to warn him," Sally said.

"But the warrior would not listen. Leviathan threw the current faster and faster like an angry flood, until the canoe stood dead."

Sally said, "Quispamsis began to cry."

"That's right, dear. Quispamsis' tears moved Leviathan, for she was innocent and beautiful and her tears soothed like a summer rain. But Pajdoobaachk shouted an insult, a warrior's challenge to one without honor, and Leviathan's anger rose beyond pity.

I could tell this was where Ghost Lady had left off, for Sally leaned forward eagerly.

"A seagull spoke with Leviathan's voice," and Ghost Lady's voice became deep and powerful, *"You have never sacrificed to me. You have lived from my bounty and never given thanks. Your spears stab the whales, my children. What then do you offer?*

"Pajdoobaachk stood in his prow. *I do not fear you, Leviathan. I skin your children for my boots and eat your fish-wives' flesh. I offer you nothing.*

"The Sky Spirit shouted a warning and the Earth Spirit groaned and split down Kloqntiej Head. A great kelp frond shot from the eye of the whirlpool and wrapped around Quispamsis' neck. *Then I claim my sacrifice,* the seagull said, and died. The Sea Spirit yanked the beautiful Indian girl from the canoe and into the murky blue. From the shore, the Mi'kmaq chiefs fell down in weeping.

"Too late, Pajdoobaachk understood his foolishness. He wailed and called on his animal guides. *Retrieve my wife for me,* he begged, and fell to his knees. *Save her."*

I envisioned the proud warrior, his face twisted in shock; the raging whirlpool; the Indians weeping on shore. The story was more real to me at that moment than anything.

"You have acted selfishly, the harbor porpoises said. *You have taken and never returned. We are your guides but we are Leviathan's creatures first of all."*

A plaintive sound came from the gravel road; I thought it was a seal. Sometimes they bark, and sometimes they groan mournfully. This was a groan.

"But Pajdoobaachk would not give up so easily. He began chanting a prayer to his ancestors. Impetuous he was, and all his strength, all his force of spirit and warrior soul poured into this one prayer – to recover his bride from Leviathan."

Ghost Lady started chanting again, this time with a subtle force that reverberated in my breast, but again there came a moaning from the road, and slowly the chant died.

That chant echoed in my thoughts long after Ghost Lady was silent. When I sail and there is only the sound of the waves lapping against the hull my diaphragm shudders in memory. I believe the Mi'kmaq ancestors would answer to it. But there on Ghost Lady's porch the low moaning came a third time and slowly I recognized the sound: the motor-driven arhooga horn from my parents' restored Model A. Somehow they knew where to find me.

"You have to go," Ghost Lady said.

I became aware of the breeze against my bare legs, the smell of rotten scallops. Reluctantly I returned from the land of the Mi'kmaq.

"You'll tell us the rest of the story, won't you?" I said.

"You don't want to spend your afternoons tending an old lady," Ghost Lady answered.

"Oh please, please tell us the end," I said. "I'll come back tomorrow. I'll bring chocolate chip cookies."

Then she smiled, and even gave my hand a squeeze. "I'll tell you the end for chocolate chip cookies, then."

I looked over to where mom and dad were waving from the car. It was loaded with picnic stuff: Frisbees, wine and food, things we wouldn't use because it was too windy. Ma always over packed.

Sally seemed to hesitate, then she pointed towards the pie tin. "Did you see anything in the bones?"

"I threw them for you Sally. What do you see?"

Sally pretended to give it great attention. "Someone is going to die," she said. "Leviathan is coming to get someone."

Ghost Lady nodded. "You are just like me, we see things."

It was my turn to elbow Sally. "Don't say things like that." I suddenly had a terrible feeling about that day.

Except for a few distant cousins that lived in Toronto, everyone I knew was at the potluck, including Sean and Timothy Maclean, who lobstered with their father from the time they could walk. They were the first boys I knew who grew beards – great, scraggly, blond things that snagged in the zippers of their storm jackets.

Motorcycle Mike cavorted near the picnic tables, spinning the smaller kids by the ankles. He hadn't earned his nickname yet but I can't think of him any other way.

Mike's sweetheart Linda Nichols was there. For the potluck, she wore a respectably long, flowery dress and braids in her hair. She brought crab cakes.

Yvonne Fourchu, the midwife, was in charge of the littler kids and the drinks. Her job was to keep all kinds of behavior in moderation.

My parents were there, of course, and Sally's, and some Smith kids we didn't hang around with, and their folks. I think they were Mormon because they had lots of food in the cellar and came from Utah and didn't drink alcohol, except rarely.

And Tom.

Tom didn't have parents, he was looked after by the Smiths but mostly by the whole town, since everybody liked him.

Oh yeah, Billy Beauregard came after it was all over. He became sheriff like his pa but he never arrested Motorcycle Mike, except for drunk driving.

First thing on arrival, Yvonne Fourchu rounded up all us kids for the usual finger waggling. It went something like this: "The ocean's really rough today, so stay away from the water. Don't go swimming and don't climb on the slippery rocks – you too, Tom. If you fall in, you'll freeze. That's called hypothermia; it can kill even the strongest swimmers."

What I really remember is Tom pinched his eyelids and pulled them inside out, and I laughed silently so Yvonne wouldn't notice. No one took these warnings seriously.

Afterwards, Tom said, "Sally, let's check out the tide pools. Last time I found a crab so big it could pinch a tin of sardines in half!"

"I have to look after Mary-Anne," Sally said.

"Squirt can come along," he said, and mussed my hair. I liked when Tom did that. He had such a cute, lopsided grin.

"We'll be on the rocks," Sally said, "playing."

Tom put his hand under Sally's chin and raised it so she was looking right into his algae-green eyes. It was terribly romantic but I could tell she didn't like it, but she let him just the same.

"I'll join you later," he said.

"Okay."

As we set up above the blowhole, I said, "Why don't you just tell him you're scared of the water?"

"Because boys don't like scared-y-cats," she replied.

"So you *do* like him."

She frowned at me in a look that meant *keep quiet*.

I didn't care much that Sally would rather be with Tom. Tom could come along if he pleased. He was off scrambling around the inter-tidal zone in that confident way of his, and in the mean time I had Sally all to myself.

I had a Barbie in my bag, Malibu Barbie I think, with the blue bathing suit. I knew Sally would pretend not to be interested, so for the longest time I didn't take it out. But we didn't have much to say, so I did.

We found a flat rock and some loose stones and kelp that we could stack into a kind of fortress. There wasn't any sand on Kloqntiej Head. The stones were damp but the tidal current was ebbing, so we weren't going to get wet. The blowhole, manifestation of the Earth Spirit's grief over Quispamsis' death, gushed like a blubbering sea serpent.

Sally and I built a little tower with a protective wall, and found a kelp bladder to play the wicked witch, which we balanced on top. Sally always made up fantasy stories to go with my dolls, so we needed a villain.

I had just proposed to search for a Ken-looking kelp bladder when a blade of sea-foam sliced over the stone-works. I squealed and stood up, but not before the back of my daisy print, summer dress got soaked.

"Look at the castle," I said. A second ripple overtook the first. The tower collapsed and the wicked witch toppled from the parapets. "It's ruined."

Seawater like an icy hand grabbed my bare feet and tumbled the purse and pink shoes I'd carefully laid aside. Then the sea pulled out, dragging the bladder-witch with it, leaving foam to bubble and pop like ginger ale. With a huff I sat on my heels and began reforming the wall…

…and felt the wrongness of it. The slate-blue Atlantic retreated, at first silently, and then with a roar it uncovered boulders and tide pools and the rift of Kloqntiej Head. The water kept going out and out and Sally and I stared at deafening emptiness.

Sally's face dropped.

I don't know how I saw that because I was looking toward the sea, but her features sagged like they were made of rubber.

Tom was gone.

Leviathan bubbled over him and yanked him from our lives.

A cold wind stung my bare arms and where my dress clung to my bottom. The adults saw where we were looking and turned to face the Atlantic and the wind froze.

We all knew he was gone.

In slow motion Motorcycle Mike struggled out of his boots and overalls and ran toward the empty sea in his long johns. He was brave that day, and I think he truly cared for Tom. Years later, when he wrote Sally from prison he would talk about Tom and how he wished he could have saved him.

Sally started to wail and that broke the spell. The men fanned out among the tide pools and my dad drove off in the Model A to get someone in town with a boat.

Sally and I were dumbstruck. We watched the men and women comb the shore but we knew there was no hope, fate was written in the bones and bloody entrails of Ghost Lady's casting. We heard someone say, "tsunami," but we knew that it was Leviathan. Nothing was going to bring Tom back. Nothing, unless...

"We still haven't heard the end of the story," I said. "We don't know it's hopeless, not for sure. Maybe Leviathan gives up the Indian girl. Maybe Pajdoobaachk finds a way to get her back, like that Greek story where—where somebody goes to Hades to play his wife back with his lyre."

I knew we were grasping at straws but Sally believed.

Without another word we tore back along the briar trails to Moody Manor. Sally must not have been running very fast because I was only a little way behind her.

Probably she couldn't breath.

My chest felt like all the air had been sucked out of it and I couldn't get anymore in except with the worst of efforts. I don't remember crying; that wave tore the tears right from my chest.

The manor looked forlorn and empty. Sally stormed to the front door and rapped the iron knocker as loud as she could. Every time we had come in the past Ghost Lady had been waiting on her porch, so I knew something was wrong.

Sally grabbed the oversized handle and threw open the door.

"No, Sally, don't," I protested. "It might be dangerous."

I held her arm but she shrugged me off. "You stay here," she said, "promise you won't follow."

I wasn't about to promise, but Sally didn't wait for an answer. She seemed to fall into Moody Manor and the door swallowed her.

I have never been so scared in my life. I stood staring at the closed door. I don't think I would have had the courage to go in except I heard a car approaching from the road and I knew instinctively we had to talk to Ghost Lady before anyone else did.

I'll never forget that place, the one and only time I went inside. Tarot cards were strewn on an antique table that could have sat a dozen; old lace hung like spider webs from the furniture. Musty animal pelts with the heads still on drooped over the coat rack where a man's cloak should have been. There was a long couch strewn with furs and I surmised that Ghost Lady slept there in the living room rather than in her bedroom.

There was an antique tub in the bathroom downstairs with griffin-claw feet, and it surprised me somehow that the Ghost Lady had running water. Mason jars filled with formaldehyde creatures sat above the marble fireplace. Upstairs there was an empty child's room with a mahogany crib and crackly wallpaper with Pan playing his flute and notes of music drifting smoke-like toward the ceiling. A half-spent candle bounced yellow off a window pane in the desolate master bedroom facing the ocean. No one was to be found; Ghost Lady had disappeared.

I found Sally staring out the bedroom window where the candle burned. Billy Beauregard's police car had arrived at Kloqntiej Head and whirled colored lights over the whole scene.

Sally leaned close to the candle, closed her eyes and whispered, "Tell me what happened to Quispamsis and Pajdoobaachk."

I never heard an answer.

That winter Sally went mad and enrolled in swim lessons.

I can't be sure about the madness.

Sally bought an aquarium and spent hours staring at the fish with a sketchbook on her knees. She wouldn't draw the fish, she would draw the thoughts the fish transmitted to her – suffocating, blue abstracts that reminded me of Leviathan and Tom. She grew extremely introverted. She didn't break ties so much as atrophy them. I can't remember her initiating a conversation for the rest of high school – she dropped below the social radar. She didn't show up the week of exams.

Fourteen years later I returned to Charlotte's Cove with a research grant in hand. An ichthyologist, I was taking measures of the decimated cod population, trying to find out why it had never recovered despite strict fishing limits.

I had lost sight of Sally while I was in university, but when I moved back Motorcycle Mike told me she lived on a 35-foot sloop called the Sea Minx. He asked me to get his abalone-shell roach clip back.

It seems his sojourn on the Sea Minx had lasted only three weeks. I suspected that Motorcycle Mike was one of Sally's longer lasting relationships.

Sally was still in love with Tom, and no real man can compete with a ghost.

It was early evening on the 14th anniversary of Tom's death. Sally and I were sailing the Sea Minx in those same Atlantic seas. We plunged into a solid wall of rain and I zipped my jacket up tight. I felt a responsibility toward Sally, otherwise I would never have sailed in such weather.

Gull Island had disappeared an hour before in a flash of lightening, and the gale cut visibility down to about 20 feet.

On helm, Sally sailed at a close reach, shouting angrily at the wind pouring over the bow.

My enthusiasm for the trip was on the lee side of wane. The Dramamine had stopped working hours ago and my stomach was now empty.

The speed crept up past 5, then 6, then 7 knots.

The boat was so heeled over that the mast sliced the tops of the swells and saltwater blasted the cockpit. I was drenched; my bare toes tried to grip the fiberglass but I had to stay seated or fall.

I hoped Sally hadn't decided to die today.

My fear grew until I couldn't keep it down any longer. "We should reef the sails," I shouted. I knew that would guarantee that Sally would contradict me, but I couldn't stay silent any longer. We should have reefed them long before.

"Hang on, we're going to see Leviathan," Sally replied, and then laughed.

That's it, she's lost it, I thought.

The 18-inch lifeline looked like a trip wire around the sloop. Sea water cascaded down the companionway into the saloon.

I struggled to open the lazarette and retrieve the hatch boards. It took me several minutes to get them fastened to keep the water out of the cabins.

If ever Sally would let me drop the sails, I was more than ready to take refuge below.

The mainsail and the jib were up. The last time I looked, the GPS chart plotter indicated we weren't near Gull Island, but the knot-meter showed we were moving fast.

I looked astern. The swells were sea monsters, writhing in windswept torment. Lightening flashed – a shadow launched from crest to trough, a canoe?

I shut my eyes, wanted to shake my head like it says in books, but that didn't help. I opened my eyes again and the canoe was gone. So was the dinghy we pulled, invisible in the tempest. The line spasmed – something still dragged back there.

Squinting through the rain – there it was, a masted canoe with a single paddler, struggling behind us.

Gaining on us?

"Sail, Mary-Anne, sail," Sally shouted. She had seen the canoe, she loved a race. "Work the lines. Let's show him what we can do."

I staggered to my feet, clung to the standing rigging and winches and anything I could and tried to trim the sails, but my instincts weren't fast enough. I became Sally's tool, responding to each command: adjusting the main sheet, winching in the jib sheets, changing the angle on the traveler...

"Do you know what day it is?" Sally asked, as I skidded from one side of the cockpit to the other. Swells broke and rain came in blinding sheets.

"You're mad," I shouted. I knew what day it was – the same day Tom had died 14 years before. "You should be put in an asylum."

"The wedding day."

"You're mad," I repeated.

Sally was going to meet her lost love.

I lunged for the helm but the deck betrayed me, sent me careening and I barely grabbed hold of the cleat where the dinghy was tied. I wrenched my wrist as I spun onto my back but I held on.

I dropped to the bottom of the cockpit and another swell rolled the sloop to port, port...

Sally let go of the wheel, raised her hands to the sky in a shout of defiance.

Maybe she blamed me for Tom drowning. Maybe she intended to give both of us to Leviathan to bring Tom back...

A mad thought burst upon me: I had to sacrifice something. Chef Boyardee Beef Ravioli; Orville Reddenbacher's microwave popcorn; salmon eggs fish bait...my mind ran through the pathetic list of offerings on board.

The canoe was gaining on us. A single warrior stove the sea with a black paddle – his sail caught the wind perfectly, responding to invisible hands. The Mi'kmaq's war paint flowed down his face in black drivels, his chant bolstered the storm.

Only a selfless sacrifice will do.

"I know the end of the story," I shouted so Sally would hear. A desperate ruse. All I could think was that I wanted to take the helm from her, turn away from the wind, reef the sails. I would deal with the warrior later – he couldn't be real, not like Leviathan and the gale.

I staggered to my knees; my frozen muscles barely responding.

I had no story to tell. What would Sally believe?

Another whitecap crashed over the side and the boat rolled so far the mast burrowed into its maw. I was wearing my lifejacket to keep from drowning and a safety harness tethered to the jack line to keep from falling overboard. Sally wore neither.

"Tell me quick, because we are going down," Sally said. The Sea Minx rolled back and fro and back again. "Leviathan wants his due."

Then the traveler broke and the boom rocketed to port; we rolled up and over. I grabbed for the wheel but came up empty and didn't remember to take a breath before we broached.

I plunged underwater.

Instantly I needed to breath but I resisted. My feet came off the deck because I was upside down.

There was luminescence. Not the blue-green glow of algae phosphoresce but true, white light. I saw Sally, wide-eyed, her blond locks surrounding her like a halo.

Everything moved in slow motion. The mast froze, pointing toward the sea floor. Then a Mi'kmaq hand broke the surface and Sally grabbed it. She reached for me with her free hand and the mast began wheeling – the sloop was trying to right itself.

I clasped Sally's fingertips but not tight enough and I slipped.

The Mi'kmaq was pulling her aboard his canoe and I kicked with all my might, closer, closer and the mast was whipping back around, I grabbed Sally's wrist and she mine and I felt the strength of the warrior as he heaved. But the sea was stronger.

The mast whipped up and the Sea Minx righted itself, and my safety harness tethered to the jack line yanked my chest so hard I nearly blacked out. I released Sally, was pulled up until I dangled chest-first from the side of the raging boat.

I managed to suck in a breath and then another half with sea water as the boat rolled and I banged repeatedly against the hull.

I coughed and sputtered but I was alive.

Lightning flashed and I saw Sally standing against the mast with her warrior, not looking back. The birch-bark canoe sliced toward Gull Island.

I've been to the labyrinth in Knossos, Crete, and you have to walk through all the twists and turns until you wind up back outside to gain meditative peace. There are no dead ends in a labyrinth, only in a maze.

Charlotte's Cove was a labyrinth, and I had walked the lanes on one side and sailed on the other, from Ghost Lady to Charlotte's Cove to the Mi'kmaq and Gull Island, and that's why I'm in Rosedown Meadows nursing home in a white, Windex-scented corridor following Ebby.

Ahead, a woman shrieks and comes shambling out of a room as fast as her walker will allow.

Ebby, not much younger than her clients, hurries forward, mumbling, "Oh Lord, what is it now, what is it now?"

Bea Clements looks out of place in the modern IKEA chair, sitting stiff-backed with her neck tall and proud. I think she is smiling, but I can't be sure.

Her room is tastefully decorated with dried flowers and posters of Diego Rivera murals that I know aren't hers, and I laugh to myself, for the nurses would never guess at the way Ghost Lady decorated Moody Manor.

"What have you done this time?" Ebby is clearly aggravated. She nervously straightens her white lab coat again and again. She says to me. "Bea is always frightening the other guests. We had to put her in a room alone, she can be so nasty. I know she's harmless, but some guests get superstitious in their old age." She waggles her finger at Ghost Lady and this reminds me of Yvonne Fourchu waggling her finger at the potluck so long ago. "What did you tell Mrs. Hern?" Ebby asks.

"I told her the phantom of Rosedown Meadows switched her Geritol for Viagra. She's all a-fluster thinking she's not going to be able to control her urges this evening."

"You didn't!" said Ebby.

"I didn't what, tell her or switch her pills?"

"You are insufferable," Ebby says. I've never heard anyone use this word in real life before. "Mary-Anne, just call if you need anything.

She can be a mischievous imp, but you just shout and Ebby will come a-running."

"Thanks Ebby," I say. I hope I get a caregiver like Ebby if my children dump me at an old folk's home.

"About time something interesting happens around here," Ghost Lady says.

Then we are alone.

There is shrieking and laughter down the hall as Ebby tries to quell the crisis. Outside the window, the sun sets orange over Charlotte's Cove and Moody Manor B&B.

Ghost Lady says, "I see you remembered the cookies."

"I've come for the end of the story," I say.

"Do you want it to be a happy end or a sad end?"

"A happy end."

"That's good, dear." Ghost Lady's eyes gleam green like a cats'. "Because that's what it is, a happy end."

The following is an excerpt from the award-winning short story, *Insect Sculptor* by Scott T. Barnes.

Insect
Sculptor

I arrived at the Hive cabaret in Abidjan, Côte d'Ivoire an hour before my audition. My only luggage, a day bag, leaned against the silver valise-insectarium marked Adam Clements. The sidewalk whirred with native people, legitimate businessmen, pickpockets, whoonga pushers barking in French and tourists of all stripes. Music blared from a divertissquirt shop. The chaos reflected perfectly my mood.

Anxiety.

I had been rehearsing the interview ever since I left Vancouver, B.C.—twenty-nine hours with layovers. I worried through another hour in an old 2038 BMW taxi that coughed at every intersection.

What would the Great Gajah-mada, the greatest insect sculptor in the world, want with me? More importantly, how could I hide the fear-wall that denied my progress?

A charming outdoor café sat opposite the performers' entrance. Further down rue Gagous the

Hive's curved-glass front bordered a fine plaza where two-meter-long bronze scorpions shot water from their claws into shallow pools. Children played in the water. Mothers in bright sarongs gossiped.

I finished my gin and tonic and ordered another, courage in a glass. My father's voice sounded in my head. "The Clements have always been engineers. Just get the degree."

No, I would not be shackled by a nine-to-five. I would return home triumphant, free from my father, free from mediocrity.

A grifter in a white shirt rolled up at the elbows picked up his coffee and sat down next to me. His arms were chocolate, his face tanned to black coffee.

"You are waiting for her? And so handsome. I know I have no chance. And yet I wait."

At five-foot-nine with mousy hair and features characterized by my sister as "knobs and bumps," I rarely thought of myself as handsome. At one time, perhaps, I imagined my gray eyes resembled Humphrey Bogart's. But at twenty-six, I had lost many illusions.

Three Vespas whined by. The grifter slurped on his coffee. "I cannot afford to see her inside the club. A month's salary for one show!"

His words began to intrigue me. Who had he fallen in love with? A waitress, I decided. They would be gorgeous and willing to indulge this gray-haired slouch for a generous tip. Poor soul. I signaled the waitress and bought him a coffee. "I am a sculptor. I seek an apprenticeship for the winter season."

"Show me something. It will help pass the time until she comes."

"You have seen the Great Gajah-mada?"

He looked surprised. "No one sees the Great Gajah-mada. But I have seen his best work. Many times."

I did not know how to take this. But I hoped the demonstration would divert me from my inner turmoil. I put the diadem-like control circlet upon my head, plugging the computer-amplifier into the socket behind my ear. My termites immediately took note, lining up at the insectarium's door.

I linked.

About the Author

A graduate of the Odyssey Fantasy Writing Workshop, Scott T. Barnes' short story, "Insect Sculptor," won second place in the Writers of the Future Contest in 2011. *Publishers Weekly* called it "lyrical."

Scott's short stories have appeared in over a dozen magazines. His fourth-grade reader *Rancho San Felipe, a Story of California One Hundred Years Ago,* with Sarah Duque, was publishing in 2013.

In addition to writing, Scott practices *kenjutsu*, Japanese sword arts. He achieved *yudansha* (black belt) with Sensei James Williams of Nami Ryū Aiki Heiho in 2013. He is writing a book on modern applications of the Samurai philosophy with Sensei Williams.

Scott is the father of two wonderful daughters, Elizabeth and Kaylynn.

More on Scott, including a complete bibliography, can be found at www.ScottTBarnes.com.

Never miss a release!

If you'd like to be notified of new releases, sign up for my newsletter. I only send out newsletters once a quarter, will never spam you, or sell your information to a third party. You can also unsubscribe at any time.

http://www.NewMythsPublishing.com/Newsletter

Reviews

It's true. Reviews help me sell more books. If you've enjoyed this story, please consider leaving a review of it on your favorite site.

www.ingramcontent.com/pod-product-compliance
Lightning Source LLC
Chambersburg PA
CBHW071229130626
46555CB00004B/1911